To my infinite mother.

PHILOMEL BOOKS

Published by the Penguin Group
Penguin Group (USA) LLC
375 Hudson Street, New York, NY 10014

USA | Canada | UK | Ireland | Australia
New Zealand | India | South Africa | China
penguin.com
A Penguin Random House Company

Library of Congress Cataloging-in-Publication Data
Van Lieshout, Maria.   Hopper and Wilson fetch a star / Maria van Lieshout.   pages cm
Summary: An elephant and a mouse set out in a lemonade-fueled airplane to fetch a star they can use as
a night-light.   [1. Stars—Fiction. 2. Elephants—Fiction. 3. Mice—Fiction.] I. Title.   PZ7.V2753Hpf 2014
[E]—dc23   2013018194
Manufactured in China by South China Printing Co. Ltd.   ISBN 978-0-399-25772-8   10 9 8 7 6 5 4 3 2 1

Edited by Michael Green.   Design by Semadar Megged.   Text set in 20-point Goudy Catalogue MT Std.
The art was created with watercolors, ink, collage, colored pencil, crayon, a smudge of acrylics and some technology to
pull it all together.

Hopper and Wilson

Fetch a Star

MARIA VAN
LIESHOUT

PHILOMEL BOOKS • An Imprint of Penguin Group (USA)

H

opper and Wilson
looked up at the
starry sky.

"I love stars," said Wilson. "I wish we had one of our own."

"It would make a great night-light," Hopper said.

"Or a lantern for nighttime adventures!" Wilson peeped.

Hopper studied the sky.
"Let's go fetch a star!"

Wilson jumped up.
"When do we leave?"

They folded their airplane, filled the tank with
lemonade, and packed their flag and a snack.

They hugged their cactus good-bye;
it was hard to let go.
"Be brave," Wilson said.
"We will be back."

The plane took off past
the trees and the clouds
into the quiet night.

"Look, Hopper!
Our cactus is just
a tiny dot!"

When they arrived at the first star,
they wandered about.
"This sure would make a big night-
light, Hopper!"

"This is not our star,
Wilson. It's too big
to carry."

They boarded their plane and
continued their search.

"Not bright enough
for a lantern."

"Too pointy for holding."

"Too sparkly for a night-light."

"Will we ever find our star, Hopper?"

"Let's take a break on the moon,
Wilson, so we can think."

The friends rested while
they ate their snack.

Wilson saw it first, the twinkly star
directly overhead that shone brighter
and clearer than all the others.

"That's our star,
Hopper!"

"Let's fetch it after
a nap, Wilson."

But Wilson was too
excited to sleep. He crept
to the edge of the light.

It was dark on the other side
of the moon.
What was over there?
He leapt into the darkness.

Wilson looked at the stars.
He let out a deep sigh.
Hopper had to see this!

"Hopper!" Wilson
looked around.
Darkness everywhere.
"Hopper?"

He shivered and walked to
the right. His teeth chattered.

He walked to the left.
It was so cold!

He looked up at a cluster of stars.
"Can one of you tell me how to get back
to my friend? We belong together!"

But the stars just hovered and twinkled.

Wilson looked up. One star shone
brighter and clearer than all the others.

Wilson swallowed his tears. "That's our star!"
His little legs darted across the dark side . . .

. . . to the bright side of the moon.
And back to Hopper.

Hopper scooped Wilson
up and hugged his shivering
friend to his soft, warm belly.

Wilson looked at the twinkling star
overhead. "Thank you," he whispered.

"I want to show you
something, Hopper."

"They are perfect, Wilson."

"They *are* perfect, Hopper, and exactly where they belong. With each other."

Plane folded for takeoff!

"I miss our cactus," Wilson peeped.
Hopper nodded. "And our home."

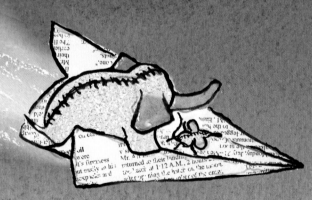

"Prepare for landing!"

That night, one star shone brighter and clearer than all the others.

"We found our night-light after all," Hopper said.

"And enough lanterns for infinite adventures!" Wilson peeped.